Ladybird Readers

Treasure Island

Series Editor: Sorrel Pitts
Text adapted by Sorrel Pitts
Illustrated by Sean Hayden

LADYBIRD BOOKS

UK | USA | Canada | Ireland | Australia
India | New Zealand | South Africa

Ladybird Books is part of the Penguin Random House group of companies
whose addresses can be found at global.penguinrandomhouse.com.
www.penguin.co.uk   www.puffin.co.uk   www.ladybird.co.uk

Penguin
Random House
UK

First published 2018
001

Copyright © Ladybird Books Ltd, 2018

Printed in China

A CIP catalogue record for this book is available from the British Library

ISBN: 978–0–241–33612–0

All correspondence to
Ladybird Books
Penguin Random House Children's
80 Strand, London WC2R 0RL

Treasure Island

To download full story audio in both British and American accents, and to complete the listening activities at the back of the book, visit www.ladybirdeducation.co.uk

Contents

Characters

Jim Hawkins

Ben Gunn

Billy Bones

Dr. Livesey

Trelawney

Captain
Smollett

the parrot

Long John
Silver

Israel Hands

CHAPTER ONE
Billy Bones

My name is Jim Hawkins. My adventure began when an old **sailor*** came to our **inn**. His name was Billy Bones, and he had long hair and a **scar** on his face.

Billy was ill. While I was looking after him, he told me stories about his life on **Captain** Flint's **pirate ship**.

"Before he died, Flint gave me a map that shows where he **buried** his **treasure**," Bones told me.

*Definitions of words in **bold** can be found in the glossary on pages 63–64.

Billy Bones died without paying his bill, so my mother and I took some money from his sea **chest**. There were some papers inside the chest, so I put them in my pocket.

That night, some strange men came and opened Bones' sea chest. Then, they became angry, and I guessed that they were looking for the papers.

CHAPTER TWO

Buried Treasure

The next day, I went to visit Dr. Livesey and his friend, Trelawney. I told them Billy Bones' story, and then I put the papers on the table in front of them.

When Trelawney saw one of the papers, he quickly became excited.

"This is a map that shows the buried treasure from Flint's ship!" he said. "We must buy a ship so we can find that treasure! Then, we must get a **crew**. Livesey, you will be the ship's doctor, and Jim, you will be our **cabin boy**!"

Trelawney bought a ship called the *Hispaniola*.

We found a good crew. Our captain was called Smollett, Israel Hands was excellent at **steering** ships, and, although Long John Silver only had one leg, he was very tall and strong, and a good cook.

Long John Silver also had a parrot that talked!

CHAPTER THREE

Pirates!

A few weeks later, Captain Smollett sailed the *Hispaniola* out of the **harbor**, and away from England. All the crew worked hard, and I often helped in Long John Silver's kitchen, because I loved listening to his stories about his adventures at sea.

One evening, I was up on **deck**, when I heard voices. Long John Silver and Israel Hands were standing near me. Their conversation frightened me.

"After we find the treasure, we'll kill anyone who won't **obey** us," said Silver.

"Kill them!" repeated the parrot.

Long John Silver was a pirate!

I went quickly to tell Captain Smollett, Trelawney, and the doctor about this conversation.

"We must attack after the treasure is found," said Trelawney, "but it will difficult, because we don't know how many pirates are on the ship."

CHAPTER FOUR

A Man on the Island

"I see land! I see land!" shouted one of the sailors, suddenly. We were near Treasure Island!

Soon, small boats took us from the ship to a beach. There were lots of tall trees on the island, and it was a dark and unhappy place. I didn't want to be there.

I walked into the forest, away from the other sailors. It felt good to be alone.

Suddenly, I saw something strange through the trees. As it came up to me, I saw that it was a man! He threw himself down on the ground.

"I'm Ben Gunn," he said. "Three years ago, I came here with a crew to look for Flint's treasure. We couldn't find it, and the sailors left me here. I built a small boat, but I can't sail it far from the island."

Then, I told him about Long John Silver and the pirates on our ship.

CHAPTER FIVE

The Hut

"It was Long John Silver who left me here,"
Gunn said. "I will help you if you take
me home."

Suddenly, I heard the sound of guns. As I
was running to see what was happening,
I saw a wooden **hut** through the trees.

Livesey, Trelawney, and the captain were
in the hut with some of the crew. There was
still a small group of pirates on the ship,
and they had the ship's boats. We could not
get to the *Hispaniola*!

"We found the hut on the map," said the
doctor, "so we can stay here."

We were all tired, and we didn't have much food to eat. We didn't know what to do.

I told the doctor about Ben Gunn, and he was very interested in Ben's story.

Then, because I was so tired, I immediately fell asleep.

CHAPTER SIX

Jim Makes a Plan

The next morning, Silver came to the hut with a **white flag** in his hand.

"If you give me the treasure map, I'll sail you to a safe place," he said.

"Leave here now, and go back to the ship!" shouted the captain, angrily.

Suddenly, the pirates attacked us! While we were fighting them, I saw the doctor run into the trees.

"Has he gone to find Ben Gunn?" I thought.

The pirates quickly became tired.
Soon, they **returned** to the ship.

"If they cannot find the treasure, Silver
and the others will sail away without us,"
I thought.

Then, I remembered what Gunn told
me—he had a small boat.

Suddenly, I thought of a plan. I was
going to sail the ship to the beach!

CHAPTER SEVEN
Jim Takes the Ship

Later that evening, I put a gun in my pocket. Then, I found Gunn's boat, and when night-time came I sailed it toward the *Hispaniola*.

As I got closer, I saw that Israel Hands was fighting with another pirate, and no one was steering the *Hispaniola*!

I sailed next to the ship, and climbed up to the deck. There, I found Hands with his shirt covered in blood. The other pirate was dead.

"I will help you if you show me how to steer the ship to the beach," I said.

I gave Hands some food, and helped him with his wounds. I thought he would obey me, but then I saw him put a knife under his shirt.

Now I knew that Hands was going to attack me as soon as the ship was on the beach!

CHAPTER EIGHT

A Fight

Israel Hands told me how to steer the ship
on to the beach. Then, immediately he
attacked me, but I quickly began climbing
up the **mast**, with him behind me.

When I reached the top of the mast,
I pointed my gun at him.

"If you come closer, I'll kill you!" I shouted.

Hands stopped on the mast near me,
but suddenly I felt his knife cut into
my shoulder!

I screamed, and kicked Hands, who fell into the water.

Then, I climbed down from the ship, and ran through the water, back to the island.

When I arrived at the hut, the doctor, Captain Smollett, Trelawney, and the crew weren't there. Then, I heard Silver's parrot, and saw Silver and the pirates through the window!

CHAPTER NINE
Silver Needs Help

"Where are Trelawney and the crew?"
I asked Silver and the pirates.

"They gave us the treasure map and went into the forest," Silver replied.

I thought that this was very strange—why didn't the crew fight the pirates? And why did they give them the map?

I didn't know where Trelawney and the crew were, so I decided to stay at the hut with Silver and the pirates.

Silver wasn't happy. I guessed that the other pirates were only obeying him because they were frightened of him.

Later, Silver came and spoke to me. "They don't like me, so they are planning to find a new leader. I promise to help you if you ask the captain to look after me," he said.

"I don't know where the captain is," I replied.

CHAPTER TEN

A Skeleton Shows the Way

Later that day, Silver and the pirates set out to find the treasure, and they took me with them! We walked through the dark forest for many hours, following the map.

"Look! A **skeleton**!" one of the pirates suddenly shouted.

"Flint has left this," said Silver. "The skeleton's hands point to the treasure!"

At that moment, we heard a strange voice coming from the trees. The men became frightened, but I knew the voice was Gunn's!

Soon, we came to a hole in the ground, but the treasure wasn't there!

The pirates were angry, and they attacked Silver. Silver turned and ran away. Suddenly, I heard guns, then the pirates ran into the trees.

I saw Silver, the doctor, Captain Smollett, Trelawney, and Ben Gunn standing inside a cave. They were holding guns!

45

CHAPTER ELEVEN
The Treasure

I walked to the cave. The treasure was there! Gunn found it after the pirates left him on the island.

We ate and laughed. "We gave the map to the pirates to lead them to the treasure," Livesey explained.

The next morning, the six of us moved the treasure to the ship, and left the island.

We didn't have enough crew to sail to England, so first, we went to South America. There, we left the ship to find more men for the journey.

When we returned to the ship with the new sailors, Gunn was waiting for us at the harbor.

"Silver has left the ship, and he's taken a small amount of the treasure with him," he said with a smile.

We left South America, and sailed home to England in the *Hispaniola*. We never saw Long John Silver—or his parrot—again.

Activities

The activities at the back of this book help you to practice the following skills:

 Spelling and writing

 Reading

 Speaking

 Listening

 Critical thinking

 Preparation for the Cambridge Young Learners exams

1 **Write complete sentences in your notebook, using *Billy Bones*, *Captain Flint*, or *Jim Hawkins*.** 📖 ✏️

    1 My name is . . . . My adventure began when an old sailor came to our inn.

    2 His name was . . . , and he had long hair and a scar on his face.

    3 While I was looking after him, he told me stories about his life on . . . 's pirate ship.

    4 . . . died without paying his bill, so my mother and I took some money from his sea chest.

2 **Listen to the definitions. Write the correct word from Chapter One in your notebook.** 🎧*

    1 crew / doctor / pirate / skeleton / gun

    2 boat / cave / hut / inn / ship

    3 flag / gun / steer / scar / treasure

    4 bury / fight / leave / return / steer

    5 arm / chest / deck / mast / pocket

*To complete this activity, listen to track 14 of the audio download available at www.ladybirdeducation.co.uk

3 **Match the two parts of the sentences. Write the full sentences in your notebook.** 📖 ✏️ ❀

1 I told them Billy Bones' story,

2 When Trelawney saw one of the papers,

3 Although Long John Silver only had one leg,

---

a he quickly became excited.

b he was very tall and strong, and a good cook.

c and then I put the papers on the table in front of them.

---

4 **Talk to a friend about the characters below.** 💬

Jim Hawkins   Dr. Livesey   Trelawney

Jim Hawkins tells the story. He is quite young . . .

5 **Read the definitions from Chapter Three.**
Write the correct words in your notebook.

1 a place where boats and ships stop   **h** . . .

2 a person who works on a boat or ship   **s** . . .

3 the floor of a ship   **d** . . .

4 one or many special things (for example,   **t** . . .
pieces of gold and silver, or money)

5 to do what someone tells you to do   **o** . . .

6 a person on a ship who steals from   **p** . . .
other people, and attacks other ships

7 a person who manages a boat,   **c** . . .
ship, or plane

8 a very large boat   **s** . . .

6 **Write a letter from Jim Hawkins to his**
mother at the end of Chapter Three.

Dear Mother,

I heard something terrible tonight! . . .

7 Listen to Chapter Four. Answer the questions below in your notebook. 🎧*📖✏️

   1 What did one of the sailors see?

   2 How did they get to the beach?

   3 Why didn't Jim want to be there?

   4 Who did he meet?

   5 When did Ben arrive?

8 Describe Ben Gunn in your own words. ✏️❓

*To complete this activity, listen to track 5 of the audio download
available at **www.ladybirdeducation.co.uk**

9 **Complete the sentences in your notebook, using words from Chapter Five.** 📖 ✏️ ✿

1   Suddenly, I heard the sound of . . .

2   I saw a wooden . . . though the trees.

3   There was still a small group of pirates on the ship, and they had the ship's . . .

4   "We found the hut on the . . . ," said the doctor, "so we can stay here."

10 **Look at the picture and read the questions. Write the answers in your notebook.** ✏️ ✿ ❓

1   Who is in the hut?

2   What is it made of?

3   What is on the floor?

4   Is Long John Silver in the hut?

5   Is it dangerous on the island? Why? / Why not?

11 **Choose the correct answers, and write the full sentences in your notebook.** 📖 ✏️ ⭐

1 The next morning, Silver came to the hut with a white . . . in his hand.
   a chest **b** flag
   c map **d** scar

2 "If you give me the treasure map, I'll . . . you to a safe place," he said.
   a bury **b** leave
   c obey **d** sail

3 "Leave here now, and go back to the ship!" shouted the . . . , angrily.
   a captain **b** crew
   c parrot **d** skeleton

4 Suddenly, the pirates . . . us!
   a steered **b** run
   c attacked **d** asked

12 **Listen to Chapter Six. Describe what happens in your notebook.** 🎧*✏️

The next morning, . . .

13 **Work with a friend. Talk about the two pictures. How are they different?** 🗨🗨

a

b

> In picture a, Jim is in a small boat.

> In picture b, Jim is on the ship.

14 **Choose the correct words, and write the full sentences in your notebook.** 📖 ✏

1 I **found / was finding** Gunn's boat, and when night-time came I **sailed / was sailing** it toward the *Hispaniola*.

2 I **saw / was seeing** that Israel Hands **fought / was fighting** with another pirate.

3 No one **steered / was steering** the *Hispaniola*!

4 I **sailed / was sailing** next to the ship, and **climbed / was climbing** up to the deck.

15 **Read the text, and write all the text with the correct verbs in your notebook.** 📖 ✏️

Israel Hands . . . (**tell**) me how to steer the ship on to the beach. Then, immediately he . . . (**attack**) me, but I quickly . . . (**begin**) climbing up the mast, with him behind me. When I . . . (**reach**) the top of the mast, I . . . (**point**) my gun at him. Hands . . . (**stop**) on the mast near me, but suddenly I . . . (**feel**) his knife cut into my shoulder! I . . . (**scream**), and . . . (**kick**) Hands, who . . . (**fall**) into the water.

16 **Read Chapter Eight. Are sentences 1–5 *True* or *False*? If there is not enough information, write *Doesn't say*. Write the answers in your notebook.** 📖 ✏️

1 Jim Hawkins left the ship.

2 He swam back to the island.

3 The crew were leaving the hut when he arrived.

4 Silver's parrot said some words.

5 Jim couldn't see Silver or the pirates anywhere.

17 **Read the answers, and write the questions in your notebook.**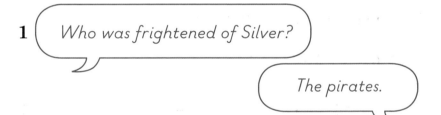

1 Trelawney and the crew went into the forest.

2 They gave the treasure map to the pirates.

3 Jim thought it was very strange.

4 Because he didn't know where Trelawney and the crew were.

5 Because they did not like him.

18 **Ask and answer the questions with a friend.**

1 *Who was frightened of Silver?*

The pirates.

2 What were the pirates planning?

3 What did Silver promise Jim?

4 Did Jim know where the captain was?

19 Choose the correct words, and write the full sentences in your notebook. 📖 ✏️ ✦

1	forest	inn	ship
2	pirate's	sailor's	skeleton's
3	one	guns	masts

1 We walked through the dark . . . for many hours, following the map.

2 "Flint has left this," said Silver. "The . . . hands point to the treasure!"

3 I saw Silver, the doctor, Captain Smollett, Trelawney, and Ben Gunn standing inside a cave. They were holding . . . !

20 Read the sentences. If a sentence is not correct, write the correct sentence in your notebook. 📖 ✏️

1 There was a skeleton on the ground.

2 Gunn was frightened of the strange voice.

3 The treasure was in the hole in the ground.

4 The pirates attacked Silver.

5 Silver, the doctor, Captain Smollett, Trelawney, and Ben Gunn were standing on top of a mast.

21 **Read the information. Choose the correct names, and write them in your notebook.** 📖 ✏️ ⬡

Ben Gunn   Jim Hawkins   Long John Silver

1   He is a young boy, and he likes adventures.

2   He is a tall pirate with only one leg, and he has a parrot.

3   He is old, and has lived on the island for three years.

22 **What happens to Long John Silver after the story, do you think? Write a new chapter in your notebook.** ✏️ ❓

After they left the Hispaniola, *Long John Silver and his parrot . . .*

Project

23   **Robert Louis Stevenson wrote *Treasure Island* in 1883. Look online, or in the library, and answer the questions below in your notebook.**

- Where was Robert Louis Stevenson born?

- Which other books did he write?

- When did he die?

- Are there any famous movies of *Treasure Island*?

- Which character would you like to be in the book, and why?

Now, work in a group to make a poster about Robert Louis Stevenson.

Glossary

bury *(verb)*
to hide something under the ground

cabin boy *(noun)*
a boy who works on a boat or ship

captain *(noun)*
a person who manages a boat, ship, or plane

chest *(noun)*
a large, strong box, often made of wood

crew *(noun)*
a team of people who work on a boat

deck *(noun)*
the floor of a ship

harbor *(noun)*
a place where boats and ships stop

hut *(noun)*
a very small building, often made of wood

inn *(noun)*
a small hotel where you can sleep, eat, or drink

mast *(noun)*
a tall part of a ship that holds the sails

obey *(verb)*
to do something that someone tells you to do

pirate *(noun)*
a person on a ship who steals from other people, and attacks other ships

return *(verb)*
to go back to a place where you have already been

sailor *(noun)*
a person who works on a boat or ship

scar *(noun)*
If you cut yourself badly, you will possibly still have a *scar* when you are better.

ship *(noun)*
a very large boat

skeleton *(noun)*
all the bones inside
a body

steer *(verb)*
to control the way a car,
plane, ship, etc., moves

treasure *(noun)*
one or many special
things (for example,
pieces of gold and silver,
or money)

white flag *(noun)*
In a war, if someone
holds a *white flag*, it
means they want to
stop fighting.